The Whale Culture in the Pacific – The Truth of the Lost Continent of Mu

Vito de la Vera

The Whale Culture in the Pacific – The Truth of the Lost Continent of Mu

My Voyages

Counterfactual Archeology

Editor: Institutio de la Vera
Proof reading: Le Club d'Aventure d'Outre-Mer
Front page picture: L'Atelier d'Aventure d'Outre-Mer
Translation: Le Club d'Aventure d'Outre-Mer

Publisher: BoD • Books on Demand GmbH, In de Tarpen 42,
22848 Norderstedt, Germany
Printing: Libri Plureos GmbH, Friedensallee 273, 22763 Hamburg, Germany

ISBN: 978-87-4305-604-1

OSAKA, JAPAN

How far your exploration can take you! My investigations began at a rock with petroglyphs on the east coast of Greenland, and now l'Aguila is sailing through the warm waters of the Pacific Ocean. I have followed the limited traces of whale culture from Greenland through Canada's Arctic Archipelago, along Alaska's coast across the Bering Sea down to the Aleutians. Here I could confirm that they really had come to the Arctic Ocean via the Bering Strait. If I had been able to explore the Siberian coast, I would undoubtedly have found traces there as well. There are at least references to rocks with petroglyphs from Vitus Bering's Great Northern Expedition. The Aleutians also clearly show that the whale culture has been here.

What clearly shows that the whale culture on the Aleutians is much older than what I found in Greenland is that there are petroglyphs under the surface of the sea. When we dived, we found far more and larger petroglyphs under the sea than above the sea. This suggests a more intensive activity over a longer period than on the rocks that are now above the surface of the sea.

This also brings the history of whale culture back to the Ice Age, and this is what we want to investigate further down in the Pacific. If the whale culture was here, their petroglyphs will be below the surface.

Fortunately, the warm water means that there have been far more dives and investigations here. Our dives in the Aleutians showed many petroglyphs that clearly connected to the whale culture. Both the petroglyphs that were above the sea in the Aleutians and also to the petroglyphs that I have found along the Arctic Ocean all the way to my first discoveries in Greenland. There is a clear connection all the way back to the underwater petroglyphs in the Aleutians, which must date back to the Ice Age, when the Bering Strait was closed and the whale culture therefore existed in the northern Pacific by the surface of the sea.

Now my goal is to investigate how far down in the Pacific the whale culture existed during the Ice Age, and this can naturally best be investigated under the sea, as the whale culture, like the Polynesian cultures, was oriented towards the sea and therefore left their traces along the coast. A coast that for the whale culture is now below the surface of the sea, as the sea level is considerably higher than during the Ice Age.

So, it's just a matter of having a starting point. The Pacific is enormous, but it turns out that I got a starting point served on a silver platter. Alain and André, who were my fellows on the test flight of our airship around Greenland, co-own an antique shop in Osaka, Japan, where they supply Osaka's wealthy with rare and special artifacts.

We visited their shop, which they run with a lovely Japanese lady, Yumiko Nakaumi, who turned out to be very knowledgeable and courteous.

It was a really exciting store with a wealth of special artifacts on 3 floors. A large space, considering the house prices in Osaka. They must be doing well.

One thing that caught my eye was a chest standing in a corner, looking very much like the one I had on l'Aguila, just older and more worn. It gave me a strange feeling, but I decided I shouldn't spend more time on it.

Yumiko served exquisite green tea and mochi. And they told us about a trip they had taken to the southern part of the Ryukyu Islands, where Okinawa is the main island. These southern islands are near Taiwan. Here they dived down to the controversial Yonaguni Monument to find artifacts that would be in demand among their clients.

During their dive, they also found petroglyphs, which they thought would interest me.

They showed us where we could find the petroglyphs and gave us 3D models that we could take pictures of to help us further. They had also taken pictures of the petroglyphs, and there were motifs that I recognized, especially the whale tail stood out. It was clear that there was something to investigate further.

During our conversation, it became clear that our friends were preparing an expedition to some of the Japanese islands in the Pacific. They didn't give details, but it was clear that they were excited. They clearly believed there was something of serious value to be found. I got a clear sense that it had something to do with the strange chest in the corner, which I kept glancing at now and then. Something I noticed our hosts also picked up on, with a strange understanding. However, we got no more from them. Business secrets, I suppose, when you have to live off your findings.

YONAGUNI, JAPAN

We spent a few good days with our hosts in Osaka before we said our goodbyes and set sail for the Yonaguni Monument. The Japanese island chain is quite long. The monument, also known as the Yonaguni Submarine Ruins, lies off the coast of Yonaguni, an island near Taiwan, and is actually disputed but under Japanese control. It took us some time to get there, but we arrived in beautiful weather for diving. It is very fitting that our investigations of the whale culture in the Pacific begin here so close to Taiwan, as it represents the starting point for the great Austronesian migration to the Pacific and thus the origin of the Polynesians in the Pacific.

When you stand on deck and look down into the clear water with a few forested islands in the background, it all looks very untouched, but beneath the surface lies the enigmatic Yonaguni Monument, which some consider to be man-made. Since the monument was last above water during the Ice Age, it was particularly interesting because it would necessarily mean that a civilization existed in such a distant past. Petroglyphs in the Aleutians also show that there was culture in such a distant past, but images from that age are known from other places.

What sets Yonaguni Monument apart is the question of whether it is natural or man-made. If it is man-made, it pushes the art of construction many millennia back into the past. When you see a 3D representation of the monument, it does resemble structures like the South American pyramids in Peru or some of the keyhole-shaped Japanese kofun burial mounds. For our purposes, it is not initially important whether the monument is man-made or natural, as long as it has been treated by human hands. If the monument is built and has petroglyphs from whale culture, it raises a whole new set of questions since there has so far been no evidence that the whale culture built in stone. In my view, it is more likely that it is a natural rock that has been shaped to a greater or lesser extent to serve a purpose.

Especially since depressions have been found in the rock, it reminds me of what I found at the whale culture's hunting sites. These depressions then served to set up tent structures. Something similar, just larger, might be the case here. An interesting thought of a large rock structure covered by large whale-skin tents. An ancient culture can identify itself in many strange ways.

However, we had to see the monument to get a firsthand idea, so it was just a matter of getting into the diving gear. The Yonaguni Monument lies at about 26 meters depth, so there is a bit of a descent, but what a sight that met us when we reached it. Before us stood a structure with straight lines and angles. It really looked like something that had been deliberately carved out. I was completely stunned; it was like seeing a monument from another world emerge before my eyes. I had to just look at it for a while. It simply filled me with awe.

After taking in the sight, we continued over the monument. We had studied the maps and 3D models, so we had a good idea of where we could find what we were looking for. First, I very much wanted to see the depressions said to be carved into the monument. After some searching, we found them. They were much larger than the depressions on the surface in Greenland, larger than I would have expected for whale culture tent poles made of whale bone. It could perhaps be for totem poles. However, we soon found smaller depressions that resembled the holes I have seen at the whale culture hunting sites. This confirms to me that the whale culture had a connection to the Yonaguni Monument, so the large depressions could be for totem poles or something else that was inside the tent structures. This might have been a ceremonial center where people gathered for cultic activities, so there must have been a larger population in the surrounding sea that could gather here.

It's interesting to imagine groups from the whale culture from the Philippines in the south to Japan in the north gathering here in a cultic community. What might they have celebrated here?

The next stop was to dive to the place where Alain, André, and Yumiko had indicated that there were petroglyphs. We swam down on the eastern side of the monument. They were obviously not easy to see, as they are just scratches in the stone. So, we had to look for a while. It took some time, but Angelo indicated first that he had found something. I hurried over.

It was indeed petroglyphs, and many of them. There was a whole gallery here. What pleased me was after some time finding the familiar whale tail symbol, which I recognized from East Greenland. It had not changed much over the millennia.

That was the evidence I needed! Along with several other motifs that I recognized; it showed that the whale culture really had been here long before it spread to the Arctic with the receding Ice Age.

Interestingly enough, we found much larger petroglyphs below the usual smaller ones. We have seen something similar below the sea surface in the Aleutians. It seems that the whale culture in the Pacific made large petroglyphs that may have been painted so they could be seen from a distance and from the air.

It is possible that they were markers for airships coming in so they could see where they were. That would make sense. We continued to investigate the petroglyphs and could conclude that they covered a large area of the Yonaguni Monument. We took pictures of as much as possible to have some documentation. Unfortunately, the sea does not allow for the kind of painting I had done above water. Here, digital enhancement of the images must be used. We surfaced again with a clear conviction that we had now followed the whale culture many millennia back in time.

Perhaps even to their cultural peak when the Ice Age made the Pacific suitable for their culture. The question is just how the Ice Age shaped the Pacific for the whale culture and how widespread it was. The question then must also be where the culture had its center, where it was strongest. Whether it was here at Yonaguni Monument or somewhere else. These are the questions we are left with. We stayed at the Yonaguni Monument for a few days and took time to consider our findings. It was clear that the Yonaguni Monument had significance for the whale culture and that it must have been an important cult center. The question was then whether we had found the core of the whale culture in the Pacific? It must have been sustained by a cold current from the Bering Sea and the Sea of Okhotsk in the north, bringing ice coverage down in the same way as off East Greenland. This provided optimal conditions for the whale culture and the whales and seals it was based on.

The culture must have covered an area from the Aleutians in the north, across the Kurils, the Japanese islands, and down across the Ryukyu Islands to Yonaguni and Taiwan. It is plausible to imagine that the whale culture spread further over Alaska and the North American coast or further south to the Philippines.

We initially had difficulty imagining that the ice current could go further towards the equator than Taiwan at that time. It was more likely that it reached the North American coast, as it even today has a cold ocean current that could have brought ice covers far south at the time. Therefore, the North American Pacific coast had to be our next goal.

Fortunately, we had something to go by. There are reports from divers about strange finds off the California coast near Los Angeles and down in Mexico near the Baja Peninsula. So that had to be our next destination. We plotted a course across the Pacific with a stop at Oahu, Hawaii before arriving in California.

It would be exciting to see if the whale culture reached as far south on the American side of the Pacific.

As I sat there contemplating aboard l'Aguila, I concluded that the Yonaguni Monument, based on what I knew then, must be a southern cult center and a hunting site for the whale culture. How much more I would learn!

Furthermore, it was my belief that the Yonaguni Monument was a natural rock that had simply been worked on by humans to serve a purpose. Those were the thoughts I had when we lifted anchor and left Yonaguni across the Pacific. It is a long journey through the vast ocean, which is the world's largest. It is day after day of blue endlessness.

Today, whales swim between the rich waters of the Bering Sea and the Antarctic Ocean, so they are always in rich waters in summer. During the Ice Age, the rich colder waters extended further south, making large parts of the Pacific more nutrient-rich.

Cold surface water leads to a significant exchange with the equally cold deeper waters, resulting in an upwelling of nutrients from the deep sea, which supports photosynthesis and plankton. Therefore, cold waters are richer than warm ones unless they are so shallow that light reaches the bottom. Therefore, the deep sea would have been richer during the Ice Ages as the cold surface water exchanged more nutrients with deeper water, leading to a plankton bloom. This plankton then drove the entire food chain up to the whales and with them the whale culture, which could have been very rich in the Pacific during the Ice Age. Cold water closer to the strong sun at the equator provided a true boom of biological activity. One can only guess how extensive the whale culture might have been under those conditions. However, the whale culture would have been bound to places where the ice came down to have a place to set down, so the interior of the ocean, where we now sailed, must have been a haven for the whales.

That's what I thought at the time without considering that the Polynesians and their catamarans were not held back from traveling across the Pacific.

We also didn't see land for long stretches. However, with modern navigation and GPS, we steadily made our way towards Hawaii, which would turn out to be the course of a detour in our journey searching for the whale culture in the Pacific. This detour would lead me to the conclusion that the whale culture was indeed the legendary land of Mu.

HAWAII, USA

We finally reached Hawaii, marking the halfway point of our journey across the northern Pacific. Thus, we arrived at the northern end of the Polynesian triangle, one of the endpoints of Polynesia's colonization of the Pacific. The other two endpoints are New Zealand and Easter Island, all areas isolated by thousands of kilometers of ocean. This made me think that if Polynesians could reach such distant places in catamarans, it was conceivable that the whale culture could fly just as far over the ocean. We needed to spend some time in Honolulu for maintenance and resupply, so I decided to investigate if there were any reports of underwater findings.

Honolulu is a city with a lovely climate, so some relaxation time here would be beneficial. However, I did not find anything suggesting there were underwater discoveries here. At least, I was unable to find any recorded reports. Perhaps the Polynesian settlement of Hawaii was indeed the first. I accepted this and focused my time on supplying and maintaining l'Aguila. At the same time, I reviewed what we had already found about the whale culture, which now stretched from the northern Pacific through the Arctic Ocean and all the way to East Greenland over a development period of several thousand years.

It turned out that I had been looking for possible observations in the wrong places. Angelo mentioned to me that among divers, surfers, and sailors, he had heard about structures and petroglyphs under the sea around Oahu. They had told him about it when he mentioned our journey. This was what we needed! Angelo had obtained the coordinates where we could dive and see what was there. We decided to take the time to sail there, investigate, and then return to continue with the resupply and maintenance work.

So, we dove down at the specified location. Fortunately, the waves around Hawaii weren't too challenging. We quickly descended along the cliffs to the plateau we had been told was underwater. It is not surprising that the whale culture is so unknown when its technology was largely based on perishable organic materials and was at sea, where it has disappeared into the depths. Adding to that the fact that the traces they left in stone in the Pacific now lie underwater, it is no wonder they are forgotten.

On the plateau, we found some indentations very similar to those at the Yonaguni Monument, but I also noticed something else. There were large stone slabs stacked on top of each other, arranged as we know from cairns. They stood at the edge around the plateau like small pillars. They were undoubtedly markers. It was the first time I had seen such cairns in connection with the whale culture, a completely new aspect I could add to my knowledge. Of course, we needed to ensure that this was indeed connected to the whale culture, which we quickly confirmed by the cliffs where we found the familiar petroglyphs. We never go wrong with whale petroglyphs!

With that clarified, we continued to examine the plateau. It ended abruptly with a drop into the depths, so it has undoubtedly been a place they flew to with their airships. It is conceivable that the cairns' function was to show where they should enter and exit the plateau. It was all very exciting but also puzzling. Hawaii is quite isolated in the Pacific, and based on what I have learned about the whale culture, they were based on hunting from sea ice, which usually forms near land and moves along the coast. So why did they end up here in Hawaii, as far from their usual hunting grounds as possible? The Polynesians sailed the ocean, so it makes sense they would reach all the islands, but the same does not make as much sense for the whale culture. There was something here that prompted reflection. I pondered this during the following time in Honolulu. How did the whale culture's presence in Hawaii fit together? Where had they come from to get here? The nearest islands lie south of Hawaii, but that made no sense considering the whale culture's dependence on sea ice.

This continued to nag at my mind, and I felt the need to investigate further. Therefore, I postponed the continued journey to California. We would head south towards the Line Islands, specifically Kiritimati. This island is relatively large and lies north of the equator. Now I needed to see for ourselves and confirm an idea that was forming in my mind.

It naturally caused some wonder that we suddenly had to search for the whale culture down by the equator, but one follows the captain's orders, and soon we left Honolulu and Hawaii, which had led me into a completely new and fantastic direction for a much deeper understanding of the whale culture and its interaction with the very special Ice Age biology of the Pacific.

KIRITIMATI, KIRIBATI

The significance of my intuition was not yet clear to me at this point. Initially, it was just the journey to the equator that mattered. The trip itself proceeded without problems, and we soon reached Kiritimati, part of the Republic of Kiribati. Kiritimati is the world's largest atoll, covering about 388 km^2 with a lagoon of similar size. If the whale culture had been at the equator and came from here to Hawaii, they undoubtedly had been to Kiritimati.

Shortly after our arrival, we went ashore to begin inquiring about underwater findings that might be of interest. Most of what we found was just vague gossip, so my optimism about my intuition quickly faded. However, it revived as we heard more and more concrete stories about something in the lagoon. Many called it the sunken city in the lagoon, which naturally piqued our interest.

Apparently, there was a shallow area in the lagoon that would be especially interesting for us. That had to be our next goal!

The following day, we set out into the lagoon to the coordinates we had been given. The weather was brilliant and the water crystal clear, so we could clearly see the shallow area when we arrived. We could actually start studying it from above. It was very interesting. There were definitely structures down there, something we were not accustomed to with the whale culture.

The residents of Kiritimati just assumed it was a Polynesian relic that had sunk into the sea. This makes sense when considering that atolls slowly erode and disappear into the ocean, and the Polynesians have left many relics in stone structures, the most famous being the monuments on Rapa Nui, also known as Easter Island, or Nan Madol. My hope was that the structure we saw beneath us was much older and belonged to the whale culture. What we could observe from above was a horseshoe-shaped depression, and to my delight, a star shape with eight triangles at the other end of the horseshoe, which I recognized from as far back as East Greenland. This filled me with great hope for what we might find down there. I made sure to sketch the shape, and Angelo then drew my attention to what appeared to be large petroglyphs around the structure, which, if painted, would have been visible from above. I was now confident that we had found yet another relic of the whale culture in the Pacific, and now even so close to the equator. This only further confirmed the growing wonder in my mind, but which I wanted to confirm further.

The next step was to dive down and take a closer look. Here, diving is a breeze with clear and warm water. We quickly descended and could confirm that it was a megalithic structure with large stone slabs set upright and large plates stacked, much like what is seen at Nan Madol. What also caught my eye were whale bones, set upright or lying down after having been toppled. Another sign that this place belonged to the whale culture.

We swam over to the standing stone slabs and quickly found they were covered in petroglyphs. It was a true treasure trove we had found here. It was almost like a library carved on stone slabs, and the joy of recognition came quickly. There was the familiar whale tail and several other recognizable petroglyphs. There was no doubt that this was a significant relic of the whale culture, far more significant than what we found at the Yonaguni Monument.

Here we had stone slabs filled with petroglyphs portraying the whale culture as a Pacific culture. Our attention was drawn to the stone slabs, where the petroglyphs formed individual images but together created a large coherent structure. It looked very unique and prompted us to study the dots and lines more closely. It soon began to dawn on us what it was, for we had something similar on l'Aguila. It was a map! Very similar to the maps the Polynesians made of sticks, where intersecting sticks indicated the positions of different islands. This was such a map, just carved on stone slabs.

It quickly became clear that there was a marker indicating our location here on Kiritimati, and from there the positions of other islands in the Pacific were laid out, up to Hawaii where we came from, and down to Easter Island and over to the nearby areas of the continents. There was Yonaguni, and interestingly enough, there was a continent in the corner opposite Easter Island. It was the sunken continental shelf, of which New Zealand is today the largest part above the water. Back then, it was significantly larger and formed a small continent!

But that is not the most exciting part! No, from what must be South America, there is a marking extending into the Pacific along and around the equator, encompassing many islands, suggesting that they are the peaks of a landmass which, as depicted on the map, forms the center of the geography. It took a moment for this to sink in. I became more convinced of the assumption I had when we found traces of the whale culture in Hawaii. There must have been something that made the central Pacific suitable for the life patterns of the whale culture—something that made it particularly suitable for whale hunting, upon which the whale culture was based. It was now clearly laid out for us. The cold Humboldt Current was the explanation! The Humboldt Current is the cold ocean current that flows from the waters around Antarctica up along the west coast of South America, turning outwards at the equator towards the Galapagos Islands. It ensures that the sea off the west coast of South America and the Galapagos Islands is colder than the latitudes suggest, much like the Gulf Stream warms Europe.

The Humboldt Current also makes the coast off Chile, Peru, and Ecuador richer in fish due to the cold water that brings nutrients up from the depths. During the Ice Age, the Humboldt Current was stronger and brought enormous amounts of sea ice with it towards the equator, resulting in drift ice in the tropics. From what the whale culture has left us here, the effect of the Humboldt Current during the Ice Age was far more extreme than previously thought. It had brought an ice cover all the way along the equator, where many of the tropical islands were surrounded by sea ice, creating perfect conditions for whales and, with them, the whale culture. The cooling effect from the ice also created favorable weather conditions for their airships, and a twelve-hour day year-round was beneficial for visibility during the hunt. The most thought-provoking aspect of the map was that the ice mass formed in the middle of the Pacific resembled many of the maps that exist of the legendary continent of Mu, which is said to have been located in the Pacific and to have been the origin of South American cultures.

Like Atlantis, Mu is said to have sunk into the sea, but where it was supposed to have been, there are no continental shelves. However, there is now an explanation: the continent of Mu was not a continent of stone but of ice! From here, the whale culture could conduct their whale and seal hunting by airship across both the northern and southern Pacific, reaching the Bering Sea in the north and Antarctica in the south. To the east and west, they could reach the Americas and Zealandia, as well as the Asian archipelagos towards the Pacific.

Another detail I noticed on the map is that the ice cover stops in the middle of the Pacific but extends to reach the northern end of Zealandia at what is now New Caledonia, where it follows the coast southwards before returning to Antarctica. The ice cover thus completely surrounds the southern Pacific and follows the southern Pacific gyre all the way around, making the southern Pacific seem like an inland sea within the ice cover.

According to the map, the northern Pacific appeared to be arranged much like the southern, but here the ice followed the west coast of America from the Aleutians down to the equator, while it was somewhat more irregular on the Asian side, where the ice seems to have gone north of New Guinea, which was part of the continent Sahul along with Australia at the time, and along the Mariana Sea to Japan and via the Kuriles to the Aleutians at Alaska. Near Japan, there was a split in the ice, which only extended down to Taiwan. The Yonaguni Monument thus formed an outer area of the whale culture's territory. The Philippine Sea was thus only surrounded by ice cover from the north and east. This is most likely a result of the influx of warmer water from the South China Sea and the Indonesian archipelago, where the shallow seas resulted in warming of the water. Southeast Asia is typically thought to have been the largest tropical area during the Ice Age, so the climate here was undoubtedly warmer.

But for the Whale Culture, this made it an uninteresting area, which is why their culture stopped at Yonaguni and Taiwan. The division of the Pacific Ocean into two large sea areas bordered by ice cover around and in the middle would also have created a very unique circulation, where water in the middle of the sea areas was warmed by the sun while being cooled by the ice cover at the rim. So, in addition to the two large rotating oceanic currents in the northern and southern Pacific that we know today, there would also have been two enormous toroidal up- and downwelling currents, where water rose in the middle of the sea and sank by the ice cover, creating an exchange of surface and deep water. This exchange would have shifted between being most intense in the north or south depending on where it was summer, as the mid-ocean would then have received the most solar energy to drive the exchange.

This means that the inner Pacific, which today is very nutrient-poor due to the lack of exchange between surface and deep water, was extremely rich in marine life during the Ice Age. This resulted in an abundance of whales. The central regions of the Pacific must have been packed with nutrients to such a degree that the Whale Culture during the Ice Age experienced enormous success, as there was ample access to their main food source, which contributed to their material wealth. From their center on the ice continent Mu around the equator, they extended along the coast north to the Aleutians and south to the Antarctic ice cover. The culture alternated between concentrating their hunting in the North or South Pacific, depending on where it was summer and thus the bloom of plankton that attracted the whales. The Whale Culture's airships could thus hover over the two gigantic sea areas to hunt. It must have been an impressive sight! With such abundance, the Mu culture must have been able to field entire fleets of airships. So many that they might almost have darkened the sky.

A thought that now takes hold of me is to what extent this abundance affected the cultural production on the ice continent Mu? With such plenty, not everyone needed to participate in the hunt; they could focus on other things. Did they only build with whale and seal skins with bones as building parts, as I saw in the Arctic, or did the Mu culture perhaps build with snow and ice, similar to what we see with the Inuit in the Arctic Archipelago? Maybe they also built large temples and buildings of ice. The Yonaguni monument could have served as a model for ice monuments on the continent of Mu. Under the southern sun and calm conditions, an entire continent of ice would have provided ample opportunities for expression, as ice is an excellent medium to work with, as evidenced by the Inuit igloos and today's ice hotels and ice sculptures.

In the Mu culture, ice would have been a very accessible material, given that the continent consisted of it. We will never be able to find anything left of all this, as a culture built from ice would necessarily melt away with the end of the Ice Age. Thus, the ice continent Mu perished as the Humboldt Current warmed at the end of the Ice Age.

It calls for reflection that the Whale Culture ultimately had to flee northward to keep up with an environment suitable for their culture, but when they finally reached so far north, they could not withstand a new cooling, as they were now in a place where half the year was dark.

The question then is whether the descendants of the Mu culture came ashore and adapted their buildings to new materials on land? Perhaps the Yonaguni Monument could have been the original model for the pyramids and monuments erected in Central and South America. It is clear, at least, that if the ice continent of Mu began to collapse, the ice cover would have survived the longest on the west coast of South America, as this is where the Humboldt Current comes up from Antarctica.

Thus, a branch of the whale culture may have sustained itself for a long time on the west coast of South America, where the more extensive works of the Mu culture could be better maintained than by the branch that went north to the Arctic Ocean via the Bering Sea. Now that I had found the main center of the whale culture on the ice continent of Mu, the next question was where the culture originated from. I had a clear picture of the subsequent development into the Holocene whale culture in Greenland and the Arctic Ocean and an idea of preservation in the South American cultures. What I did not have a clear picture of was where the Mu culture had come from to their ice continent. However, I had my considerations. As I mentioned, the Yonaguni Monument, which I believe is mostly natural but carved by humans, could have been an inspiration for the ice architects on the continent of Mu and subsequently for pyramids and monuments in clay and stone in Latin America. This implies that the whale culture started out in this area and from here became the Mu culture.

My thought is that they came to Yonaguni from the north over the ice along the Ryukyu Islands. Hence, Japan must have been the starting point for the spread of the whale culture across the Pacific, just as it was the starting point for my search for the whale culture in the Pacific.

What do I base this expectation on? It seems to be the most likely, as America was first populated around the same time that the Mu culture had reached its peak, and further south in Asia, there were warm seas between the ice and the mainland. Japan, on the other hand, borders the Sea of Okhotsk, which was ice-covered, and on the other side of the Japanese Sea lay the Asian part of the Mammoth Steppe, where hunter-gatherer cultures lived off the steppe's rich megafauna. A group of these mammoth hunters could have settled at the edge of the ice from the Sea of Okhotsk and used it to cross over to Japan.

At the same time, their proximity to the coast and the ice meant they could start hunting marine mammals like seals and eventually whales. The ice also provided protection against many of the dangerous predators that lived on the Mammoth Steppe. On the water, only the polar bear remained a threat. Therefore, it is most likely that the whale culture developed in Japan after crossing over from the mainland. On the Japanese islands, the culture also had the opportunity to reach the northern Pacific area, which was extremely productive waters at the time. Therefore, it is also most likely that the whale culture first saw the light of day here.

Subsequently, the culture spread over the ice southwards to Yonaguni and Taiwan, where the ice did not extend further, but they found the then-dry Yonaguni Monument and carved it so that it could serve as a kind of sanctuary at the edge of the ice.

Similarly, the culture could have followed the ice north to the Aleutians and from there down along the North American coast. But it was the ice-covered route down along the Marianas from Japan that brought the whale culture to its peak, as they reached the large ice continent in the middle of the Pacific, where their culture could reach its zenith. All of this became apparent to us as we examined the stone slabs in the lagoon on Kiritimati. There was enough here for a longer period, so we anchored and prepared to stay. We launched the small boat so we could sail into town and provision when necessary. It was a lovely place, so it did not matter that we had to be here for a while.

We took daily diving trips down to the stone slabs to study the petroglyphs. It quickly became clear to us that Kiritimati had been at the center of the Mu culture. It is interesting to consider that the Line

Islands, which are now remote from everything, were during the Ice Age the center of a highly developed culture based on hunting rather than agriculture.

The petroglyphs here are much more advanced than what I have previously seen in the Aleutians, Greenland, and the Arctic Ocean. This was clearly a culture with far greater resources at its disposal. The rows of stone tablets also testify to this; the Mu culture has created a memory of its existence for posterity here. They were aware that something had to be done in stone rather than the fleeting ice, which flowed with the current and melted away. From our interpretation of the petroglyphs, it became clear how advanced the Mu culture had been. It certainly had the airships and advanced blubber lamps with heat and propulsion that I know from the whale culture, but that was only the beginning.

Like the Inuit, they built in ice, creating entire cities on the ice continent of Mu, where they carved buildings out of ice and built them from ice blocks, furnishing them with skins from whales and seals. It was a constant building process since the buildings slowly melted, so new buildings were constantly being constructed to replace the old ones.

Ice blocks were lifted into place by airships functioning as cranes. Snow served as mortar, locking the ice blocks together. Inside the buildings, it was cooler than outside, but if it got too cold, the blubber lamps could be used for heating and light at night. Since the buildings were made of ice, they allowed the sun's light to stream in during the day, so it was always bright inside. If dark rooms were desired, they could be made with skins or snow. The stone tablets turned out to reveal an entire archive of the Mu culture's daily life. They clearly showed how they alternated between the northern and southern Pacific according to the seasons. They showed their building techniques and the use of whales for their technical and practical purposes. There was an overview of the whales' migration patterns between the south and the north. These migration patterns were immensely important for the whale culture.

It is clear from the petroglyphs that the whales' migration over the year was not as long as it is today, as they did not have to travel so far to find abundant plankton blooms in the then-rich Pacific Ocean. One symbol that still stands out is a stylized figure-eight, which is the Mu culture's symbol for their world. The ice cover forms the lines of the figure-eight, while the holes are the open areas surrounded by ice in the northern and southern Pacific. The Mu culture had a good overview of the shape of their world. In the north, this world was dominated entirely by ice and Asia and North America, while in the south, there was another side of the ice, south of Zealandia, where the culture may have been able to follow the southern side of the Indian Ocean and into the South Atlantic until they reached the ice that extended up around the southern tip of South America. The big question is whether part of the whale culture in this way made the journey around Antarctica. There is nothing in the petroglyphs that immediately confirms this, but they were at least along the ice edge in the southern Pacific.

Is it possible that part of the whale culture moved down to Antarctica at the end of the Ice Age in the same way they moved up into the Arctic Ocean during the Holocene maximum? Of course, we cannot answer this from stone tablets from before the end of the Ice Age, but it opens new possibilities for future investigations. The southern tip of South America at Tierra del Fuego could also have been a place where the whale culture kept its whaling alive for a long time without changing to other sources of sustenance. Thus, the stone tablets give rise to a true flood of thoughts that I had not considered when I first examined petroglyphs on the rock in East Greenland. What an adventure it has sent me on, finding the traces of the continent of Mu!

We find petroglyphs that also show the large hunting fleets of airships that set out over the sea. They continually returned home with rich spoils, keeping the Mu culture going.

Airships were also sent out to map the ice edge as it developed and even a bit into the continents, where conditions allowed. Particularly

South America, where the Humboldt Current came from, seemed to be of interest.

The peaks of the Andes are clearly shown in the petroglyphs. The Mu culture was aware of where the basis for their culture, in more than just a figurative sense, came from. It therefore also makes sense that they flew their airships toward the Andes. However, given how dependent they were on the sea, it is doubtful that they crossed them, but they could probably get up to the Altiplano and perhaps to Lake Titicaca, which might have been of interest.

Given how much the Nazca culture's geoglyphs resemble the large geoglyphs I found underwater in the Aleutians, it is very likely that the high cultures in Latin America descend from the Mu culture, which came ashore here when the ice disappeared.

Their petroglyphs and geoglyphs have been preserved in cultures such as the Nazca, and with a culture with airships, the large Nazca lines, which can only be seen from the air, also make sense. Given that the Humboldt Current on the west coast of South America kept the waters cold and nutrient-rich here, the whale culture's way of life could also survive along the coast without suffering the same fate in the winter darkness as the whale culture in the Arctic Ocean. Likewise, many of South America's pyramid temples also bear resemblance to the Yonaguni Monument, so just as the ice temples on the continent of Mu were inspired by the Yonaguni Monument, the temples in South America continued this tradition after they were forced ashore. In South America, the Mu culture would likely have had the opportunity to gradually evolve away from the whale culture's dependence on the sea without completely collapsing in the process. It is therefore becoming increasingly clear to me that the Mu culture and the whale culture were the original colonizers of America, both in the form of those who would become the Inuit and the indigenous peoples.

Therefore, there may be much to suggest that parts of America were populated from the south by parts of the Mu culture that landed in Peru. It is becoming increasingly clear that we should look for the future of the Mu culture and the whale culture in Latin America, while its past should be found in Japan and Taiwan. There is also much to suggest that the Ainu people in Japan are the last remnants of the whale culture here, which were displaced when the rice-growing Yamato people, who formed modern Japan, arrived. In Taiwan, the remnants of the whale culture became the Austronesian people, who would repopulate an ice-free Pacific in the form of the Polynesians and reach all the way to their distant relatives in America to spread the sweet potato across the Pacific islands. Thus, the distant descendants of the whale culture have returned to their ancestors' home in the Pacific, where fewer of the islands are now above water.

It is a satisfying thought that the descendants of the Mu culture still live here so long after, under very different conditions. Now, only the islands that once stuck up above the ice remain. While we have studied the tablets and let our thoughts wander regarding where the Mu culture developed from and to, the idea has arisen that we should try to descend from the lagoon and explore the coast and coral reef at the Kiritimati atoll to see if there are geoglyphs like those in the Aleutians, which could show a connection to the Nazca culture in South America. We decide to make the attempt and sail out, where the depths extend beneath us near the shores of the atoll. It is strange to think that the deep water beneath us was once covered by a layer of ice that stretched across the Pacific as an entire continent. We jump in and begin our investigations of the atoll's sides, which extend down into the depths. Initially, we do not make any significant discoveries and must return disappointed to l'Aguila.

We try for several days without success but then get the idea that we should search at the entrance to the lagoon, which previously served as a gateway over the ice. So said, so done! We position ourselves at the opening of the lagoon and dive down where the lagoon drops into the depths. Here, there are some large surfaces that were above water when the ice masses surrounded the island. It must be said that it is not easy to find geoglyphs underwater! The visibility leaves much to be desired.

Fortunately, the sea at Kiritimati is much clearer than the sea at the Aleutians, so we can see much better. But even then, it is a task that requires patience. We now swam back and forth at a distance where we expected to see lines on the surface if there were any. It is a large area, so we did not find anything in the first few days, but then we succeeded! We spotted some markings that looked very unnatural. We could not see what they depicted but swam over and followed the markings up close.

It was not surprising that it had been a challenge for us to find anything. This geoglyph was enormous! To see the whole thing, we would have to move further out, but then we wouldn't be able to see the lines. So, other solutions were needed! We swam at a distance where we had an overview and took pictures of the surface. Now it was just a matter of returning to l'Aguila. We transferred the pictures to the computer and used artificial intelligence for pattern recognition. A fantastic tool for finding what one cannot see oneself. It certainly found something. It was not just the geoglyph we had discovered. There were several remarkable geoglyphs under the entrance to the lagoon. There was a clear sun, an airship, the familiar whale tail, and human figures resembling those known from the Nazca culture and other Peruvian cultures. The Mu culture thus had a tradition of making geoglyphs in the same way as seen in South America.

These geoglyphs must have been an impressive sight for arriving airships gliding over the ice landscape to see the atoll rising above the sea with large, undoubtedly painted geoglyphs. There is no doubt that something in the geoglyphs told the airship travelers where they had arrived. Since the islands were the only fixed points in the moving ice continent, they undoubtedly served as markers indicating where one had arrived and which direction to take to other islands.

The thought that strikes me is that the Mu culture may also have made geoglyphs on the ice. But these would have been as impermanent as the buildings. However, they would have been much easier to make. All they needed was hot water and perhaps a bit of dye. Both could be taken from their prey and their powerful blubber lamps, which they could use to fly in airships, should have been able to produce hot water in large quantities. Thus, they should have been able to make ice geoglyphs.

Airships from the Mu culture could thus have followed ice geoglyphs on their journeys over the ice continent Mu. Since the whale culture based their airships on materials they could take from whales, they could produce enormous quantities of airships during the Ice Age based on the number of whales available. It must have been far more impressive than what I observed of the whale culture in Greenland, which did not have the same wealth available. The importance of airships as a means of transport is also clearly seen from the large geoglyph of an airship that adorns the screen after the artificial intelligence has drawn it up. However, there is more that catches my eye. Among the geoglyphs is, of course, the familiar whale tail symbol I saw in Greenland, but there are also other whale figures along with human figures where it is not a hunting motif.

No, on the contrary, it looks like there is a collaboration, with some figures appearing to show the Mu people riding on whales, perhaps dolphins, and larger. They did not only hunt the whales but tamed them!

It is an incredible thought and not something I have seen in my findings from Greenland, the Arctic Ocean, or the Aleutians. It must be something that was forgotten with the downfall of the ice continent. When you think about it, it actually makes sense. Despite the ice, the water and climate was somewhat milder here under the equatorial sun, so the Mu people have been better able to endure being in the water. Therefore, interaction with whales in the water has also been more possible than in the icy waters of the Arctic. This gives a completely new picture of the Mu culture, involving a much closer relationship with whales. We must return to the stone tablets in the lagoon to see if we can find petroglyphs that can show us more about this interaction with whales.

The next day we are back at the site in the lagoon where the stone tablets stand in the water beneath us. We need to take a closer look at the many petroglyphs that cover their surfaces. Here we hope to find petroglyphs that can tell us more about the Mu culture's interaction with whales and what it meant for the culture at its peak. We already know that they were entirely dependent on whales for their material needs, but were whales also a kind of domestic animal and partners? We dive down and soon begin examining the stone tablets and petroglyphs. A clear picture soon begins to form. We see people strapped to what must be dolphins being used as mounts, swimming through the water. There are races and battles from their backs and many sports that take place this way.

To my surprise, there are also sleds being pulled through the waves in the same way dogs would pull a sled in Greenland. These sea sleds have a team of dolphins in front, and the runners are a form of surfboards with seats on top, one surfboard on each side like a sled. There are also petroglyphs depicting whale hunting, where the Mu people in their airships collaborate with orcas to capture large whales. This is reminiscent of what was known from Eden in New South Wales, Australia, where whalers and Aboriginal people worked with orcas in whale hunting. It appears that it was common for the Mu culture to collaborate with orcas, and we therefore find petroglyphs showing orcas in a way that signals affection. The Mu culture thus seems to have been a pinnacle of collaboration between whales and humans, even though the culture was also dependent on whales for materials.

It appears that it was primarily dolphins and orcas that the Mu culture lived with. It also seems that orcas were used as draft animals for airships. In those cases, the blubber jet was only used to heat the air in the balloon, while a harness connected to an orca pulling the airship over the sea. This was an effective way to save fuel for long journeys over the ocean. The airship crew likely also collaborated with orcas to catch prey when the opportunity arose. There are also petroglyphs showing the blubber lamps used for the airships' blubber jet. It is a whale bone that had been hollowed out and bent so that the air intake bends downward while the exhaust goes horizontally to provide propulsion.

Inside is another strongly perforated tube that brings air all the way through when the surrounding tube is filled with blubber. The fire is lit at the back, starting the air intake from the downward end. When the blubber is well-heated, it rapidly draws air into the burning blubber and up through the entire length. This creates a powerful jet that comes out of the exhaust. It was strong enough to propel the airships forward and keep the balloon warm enough for lift. At the same time, the blubber lamps were used for many other purposes. Among other things, they seem to have been used to carve figures out of blocks of ice. Additionally, they were used for point heating of stones to create depressions for posts and totem poles, as well as the large geoglyphs. It was indeed a valuable tool, which was crucial for the abundant whaling that the Ice Age Pacific provided the Mu culture.

The whale was thus the all-important resource for the whale culture, with the seal being the second most important, also used for clothing. Seal skin, as in the Arctic, formed the basis for clothing in the Mu culture since they had very limited access to plant fibers. There was undoubtedly a use for every part of the animal, both whale and seal. Again, the fact that so much of the Mu culture and the associated whale culture was based on organic material means that very little has been preserved for posterity, and what could have been preserved undoubtedly lies at the bottom of the sea, where it is unlikely to ever be found. Like the later whale culture in Greenland, it seems that the Mu culture's burial rituals involved giving the dead to the depths of the sea, so countless generations of the whale culture now rest in the depths of the Pacific Ocean. When considering how extensive the Mu culture was, it has left very few traces.

It simply disappeared with the climatic conditions that made it possible, and very little has been remembered among its descendants on land. Only what has been carved in stone remains, and this seems to have been preserved among the descendants in the Nazca culture. As we examined these stone slabs, there was much that suggested our next stop should be the coast of Peru in South America, where we would see what traces we could find of the branch of the whale culture that must have retreated there as it withdrew from the Pacific. At least, that was my expectation until my eye fell on yet another petroglyph, a variation of the maps that had previously given us an idea of the figure-eight-shaped ice cover that had existed in the Pacific.

This map, however, highlighted something else. Zealandia, the submerged landmass of which only New Zealand and New Caledonia are above water today, is brought more into focus here. It is highlighted as if it has a special significance! It piques my curiosity. Why is Zealandia highlighted when the Mu culture was based on the sea and ice? I needed to study this connection more! During the Ice Age, Zealandia was an elongated continent that had the large Pacific ice to its east. Before the Ice Age, like today, the continent was submerged except for New Zealand and New Caledonia. Conversely, these two areas would have been covered in glaciers. Perhaps not entirely New Caledonia, but much of what was above water before the Ice Age would have been under ice during the Ice Age. Zealandia must therefore have been a fairly blank slate during the Ice Age, populated by the animals and plants that could reach it or had survived from before the Ice Age. Some of those seem to have influenced the whale culture. The question is, what did this continent offer them that gives it a prominent place on the stone slab?

It must have been of some interest, even though it might have been one of the last places in the Pacific they reached. The continent could have had two faces simultaneously, with the Pacific side covered in ice, but on the side towards Australia, which was then land-connected with New Guinea in the continent Sahul, there was a relatively enclosed inland sea that must have been significantly warmer. Zealandia would thus have had a cold and a warm side over a relatively short distance. Since the whale culture thrived mostly where there was ice, it is puzzling that this continent was interesting beyond the cold end, which also existed elsewhere around the Pacific. However, it is noteworthy that there was a warm sea with humid air on the western side, which must have been important! The stone slab contains many petroglyphs that refer to precipitation. It can be assumed that the warm humid air was carried over and brought a lot of precipitation over the mountain range of Zealandia and down over the ice cover.

Zealandia may therefore have been a driver in the continuous influx of ice and snow in an otherwise dry Ice Age. From Zealandia's coast, the extensive precipitation would have followed the ocean current down towards Antarctica and then joined the Humboldt Current along South America's Pacific coast. Thus, the sea between Zealandia and Australia would have been a relatively closed, warm inland sea that contributed ample precipitation to form ice in the Pacific circulation.

It appears that the Mu culture at its height was well aware of this ice-producing mechanism. Therefore, Zealandia had a central place in the culture. The question then is whether it was a breakdown in this mechanism at Zealandia that led to the demise of the figure-eight-shaped ice cover in the Pacific and the continent of Mu sinking into the waves. The stone slabs do not say. They contain knowledge from the height of the Mu culture, not its downfall. However, it is to be expected that when the ice cover weakened, it happened quickly. Much faster than the melting of the continental glaciers. The solid ground beneath the Mu culture's feet simply melted away. I wonder how they reacted to that? They must have retreated to the solid footholds that the islands provided, but here the subsequent melting of the continental ice caused sea-level rises that submerged most of the works the Mu culture had built. Even the Yonaguni Monument disappeared into the depths. Presumably, the whale culture followed the ice back to always be where the best conditions were. They must therefore have moved up along the coasts of Japan and North America towards the Arctic and over towards the coast of South America where conditions were better. But what about Zealandia? How long were the conditions on the Pacific side good here, and what about down towards the Antarctic ice cover?

How long could the whale culture survive here as they did in the Arctic? In the Pacific, they might have been able to survive for a while without ice. What really made the difference was the collapse in the exchange between surface water and bottom water that the ice cover facilitated. Without that, nutrients did not come up, and the Pacific turned into today's oceanic desert with nutrient-poor water. That was the blow that ended the Mu culture in the Pacific. After that, it could only continue by the Bering Sea and along the cold Humboldt Current along South America and out to the Galapagos Islands. These islands might therefore be a good place to find signs of the late whale culture in the Pacific. However, it is Zealandia that still holds my attention. This precipitation pump was crucial for the whale culture's world, so it is interesting what presence they had here and what development took place when the precipitation system ceased.

After some consideration, we decided that this would be our next goal. We weigh anchor and see what we can find at New Zealand, where the highest peaks of Zealandia were found. The next day we set sail from the harbor in Kiritimati. This island has told us more about the Mu culture than we had dared to hope. We have plenty of records with us to study further when our journey is over for this time, but first, we need to follow through on our discoveries. As we sail towards the western corner of the Polynesian Triangle, we have plenty of time to start studying nautical charts and depth maps of the seabed at the now mostly submerged Zealandia.

It is an enormous, predominantly submerged continental shelf extending east of Australia and covering a comparable area. Our studies of the maps will hopefully give us some ideas of where it would be good to search for petroglyphs from the Mu culture. At the same time, we also look for reports of finds in New Zealand that could point us in the right direction.

TAHITI, FRENCH POLYNESIA

On the way to New Zealand, we decided to stop in Tahiti, French Polynesia, to resupply and take a break to digest our discoveries before continuing our journey. At the marina in Papeete, however, our journey took a new turn when I spotted a yacht I knew so well. It belonged to Jacques Pierre, another member of Le Club d'Aventure d'Outre-Mer. We have often crossed paths. He can be unbearable and very French, but he keeps me on my toes, and when you know a fellow club member is nearby, you must show courtesy and pay a visit. It turned out that Jacques was traveling with the writer Kai Kean, who was apparently writing about his travels and interests.

They were somewhat secretive, but it didn't bother me much. I chose to be more open and told them about our journey and discoveries. I know Jacques has never thought much of my work on the whale culture, but he was surprisingly receptive. He let me know that on his trip to New Caledonia, he had found something underwater: a megalithic structure with petroglyphs and worked stones. This was, of course, very interesting to me, and he kindly provided me with the coordinates of his discovery.

This was quite significant since New Caledonia is the northernmost end of Zealandia. Following this meeting, we decided to change our plans and head to New Caledonia instead of New Zealand. We still spent a few days in Papeete, and Jacques Pierre proved to be an excellent host for some extra socializing. When we set sail, he even wished us "bon chance" on our journey.

It shows that sometimes a rival can also be a friend when you are not on each other's turf. From Tahiti, our course then took us to New Caledonia, leading us from one French overseas territory to another across the vast expanse of the Pacific. The Pacific is so enormous that it truly feels like a different world. The world we know seems infinitely distant. This is a world of ocean, and a continent of ice could easily have existed here and still remained hidden from everyone.

One must admire the Polynesians who sailed these endless expanses without any sight of land. The whale culture, in its time, at least had the ice. The Polynesians only had the many small and isolated islands, each a world unto itself, isolated from the rest of the world by the infinity of the ocean. Like small planets separated from each other by the infinity of space. If we want to get an idea and training on how space colonization will be, we just need to look at the Polynesians' colonization of the Pacific.

They were small groups of people isolated on small vessels in a unique and hostile environment in search of just a little rock to set foot on. Does that not sound much like what future space colonization will be and has been so far? And each little island is its own world, as New Caledonia, where we are now headed, is an excellent example of. This archipelago constitutes a lost world in itself, filled with animals and plants that form their own unique families and genera on the tree of life. They have existed in unique isolation for millions of years and are thus a relic from the supercontinent Gondwana, much like Australia, but with a longer and more isolated history. New Caledonia is therefore likely a good image of what the whale culture would have encountered on the lost continent of Zealandia, where they found the mechanism that kept their ice world in the Pacific alive.

NEW CALEDONIA

It is this world that we are now approaching after our long journey across the Pacific. We are heading towards Nouméa, the capital of New Caledonia, from where we will set out to the coordinates that Jacques Pierre kindly provided us. Nouméa is a charming French-influenced city located on a peninsula of New Caledonia's main island.

Once we arrived and docked at the marina, we decided not to immediately head out to Jacques Pierre's coordinates after provisioning. Instead, we planned to rent a car and explore some of New Caledonia's landscape. This would give us an idea of the conditions that the Mu culture might have experienced on the warm side of Zealandia. The vast majority of New Caledonia's flora and fauna is endemic and found only here, so it would be similar to what the whale culture encountered if they had traveled away from the ice in the east to find the warm inland sea in the west.

At the same time, New Caledonia is geologically very old. It is the original primordial rock from the supercontinent Gondwana, which protrudes here with a wealth of minerals. New Caledonia alone accounts for 40% of the world's nickel production. That puts the mineral wealth into perspective! As we drove through the tropical landscape, it suddenly felt as if we were moving through a lost world.

It's like a small fragment from the age of the dinosaurs or at least a glimpse of how life might otherwise have evolved. Zealandia truly is a distant fragment even further away than Australia, where life evolved in its own unique direction. Together with the ice continent Mu, the establishment of the Mu Culture on Zealandia and the subsequent flooding of the continent was also the downfall of the Mu Culture, with Zealandia's submersion marking the final and definitive end of the great, nutrient-rich ice world in the Pacific. It was truly an entire world that vanished, leaving behind only small fragments such as here in New Caledonia.

With New Guinea and Australia united into the continent of Sahul in the west and Zealandia in the east, there was a large inland sea in between, which was narrowly connected to the sea between the Philippines and the Marianas to the north and down to the South Sea and the ice cover in the south. If the water flow was primarily from the north, which is not unlikely since the water's only other outlet was the strait between the Sunda Islands, which then was the Sundaland Peninsula, the water would have come in warm from the north, much of it evaporating and moving east over Zealandia or Mu, if you prefer to call it that, and falling as precipitation in the form of snow on the other side of the mountains as it cooled down.

What remained of the ocean current would then have flowed into the circum-Antarctic current, which was entirely covered by ice at that time. The Pacific Ocean was generally quite isolated during the ice age, with the Bering Strait being land and the Sundaland Peninsula closing off Southeast Asia. There was only the strait between Sahul and Sundaland, leading out into the Indian Ocean; otherwise, there was the warm sea between Sahul and Zealandia and the flow down into the Antarctic South Sea from the Southern Pacific, which was also open to Antarctica and the Circum-Antarctic current.

Thus, the Pacific Ocean was a relatively closed system, largely isolated from the rest of the world by the ice of the ice age. In this closed oceanic world, a fragment of the supercontinent Gondwana existed, leading an isolated existence with its own unique flora and fauna, evolving separately from the surrounding world.

This mysterious world was what the whale culture found on Zealandia, arriving at a familiar ice world on the eastern side but discovering a warm, tropical prehistoric world on the western side that could not be more different from what they had come from. I wonder what effect finding such a different world had on them?

For us, it was certainly an experience to be exploring New Caledonia's strange landscape and nature. It would be an ideal place to film alien worlds. And it is, after all, a French overseas territory.

In any case, New Caledonia, along with New Zealand, would have represented the highest areas of Zealandia, forming a sharp boundary to the Tasman Sea, which would have been significantly less connected to the Pacific and nearly an inland sea between Sahul and Zealandia. This created the conditions that allowed the Tasman Sea to be a warm sea with evaporation, while the Pacific Ocean remained cold and suitable for the whale culture.

On the other hand, the Tasman Sea would have been far less suitable, and the warmer air would have reduced the buoyancy in the airships that the Mu Culture used. So, it is interesting to consider how far west on Zealandia the Mu Culture might have traveled.

I can't help but notice that the coordinates Jacques Pierre gave me are on the western side of New Caledonia. This means it is on the warm side of the highland that New Caledonia was in Zealandia. That gives food for thought. The Mu Culture must have explored the continent that was such a crucial piece in maintaining the ice cover in the Pacific. They even explored it so thoroughly that the connection was known even in the center of the ice continent, at Kiritimati.

What interests me now is how the Mu Culture evolved on Zealandia, where they encountered a climate very different from the one their culture was based on.

They must have spent a long time on Zealandia; otherwise, knowledge about it would not be as widespread as it is on the stone tablets in Kiritimati. Therefore, they must have adapted in a direction suited to Zealandia's conditions. Hopefully, it will provide some answers when we head out to the coordinates on the west coast. The day after our little detour, we set out for our primary objective here in New Caledonia. It was only a couple of hours' sail before we dropped anchor at the coordinates in a calm sea, perfect for diving.

I must admit I was excited about what our diversion from the planned trip to New Zealand would reveal. Jacques Pierre had mentioned many megalithic structures under the sea and numerous petroglyphs, so I had high expectations as I put on my oxygen mask and let myself fall backward into the water.

The water was beautiful and clear. A clear sign that it was nutrient-poor but good for visibility. Then, the sunken city revealed itself to me. I was breathless. Jacques Pierre had not exaggerated, quite the opposite. Beneath us was a large area with megalithic structures and regular stone slabs. It wasn't just isolated megaliths but gigantic structures like Stonehenge and entire walls built of basalt blocks like Nan Madol. I had not anticipated anything like this from the Mu Culture. I could only imagine what they might have been able to build on the ice continent. I tried to imagine these buildings covered with their whale-skin tents. It must have been an impressive sight, much like the Yonaguni Monument. This city lay just on the other side of the ridge that New Caledonia represented on Zealandia, facing the warm plain and the warm Tasman Sea.

It must have been one of the first sights that airships coming in from the Pacific encountered as they passed New Caledonia's highlands. Now I am eager to learn what led to the construction of a city in stone, which was unfamiliar to the Mu Culture. We came down and swam among the megaliths. It is an impressive sight in the clear water. The most important thing for us, however, is to find petroglyphs that can tell us something about this strange city, where the whale culture took a significant leap in a direction, they did not retain in the later Holocene whale culture that I once discovered in Greenland. What we see here is undoubtedly also the result of a local development of the Mu Culture that did not spread much outside Zealandia. My thoughts are interrupted by Angelo, who catches my attention and points towards what turns out to be stone slabs similar to those we found in Kiritimati.

It is almost like the whale culture's version of a library. We approach the slabs. The water is so clear that we can see clearly that they are covered with petroglyphs. We quickly find much that confirms what we have already seen in Kiritimati, Hawaii, and Yonaguni, but what we are really looking for is something more detailed that can tell us about this city, now that we know it belongs to the Mu Culture. It takes us some time, but we finally find some slabs with clear local motifs. It is evident that the images depict a warm sun over a lush tropical landscape. What stands out, however, is that they show airships from the Pacific arriving with trade goods, skins, bones, and everything else that the whale culture could offer, and in return, they receive gifts here in the city. What stands out is that the most important items given in return for whale products here in the city were feathers and feathered garments.

New Caledonia and New Zealand are rich in unique birds, and Zealandia must have been the same. The many colorful feathers found on these birds were highly prized in the Mu Culture. They were the warm part of Zealandia's great trade goods! The Mu Culture, like the Native American cultures in Mexico and Peru, was fascinated with feathers and used them as status symbols and signs of wealth. It makes sense that colorful feathers would have been prized in a white ice world.

Zealandia could supply these sought-after feathers! This is how the city became important and powerful. It was a source of luxury goods for the Mu Culture. Beautiful feathered garments were undoubtedly highly sought after throughout the Mu Culture, and now that we have seen it, many petroglyphs we had seen earlier begin to make more sense. The problem is that no colors are preserved in the petroglyphs. We simply could not see that they depicted feathered garments!

In addition to feathers and feathered garments, colorful shells and corals from the warm sea were also an important trade good. This suggests that this city must have been able to import large quantities of whale meat and other whale and seal materials from the broader whale culture.

It is becoming increasingly clear that the whale culture had impressive activity in the warm Tasman Sea. Just like in the colder Pacific, their vessels were dragged by tame dolphins and orcas, the petroglyphs here show that they actively rode on whales, as the water here was warm enough to be in. It also seems that they used local reeds to make reed boats, which the whales pulled out to the corals, where they would then dive and harvest the valuable corals and shells that contributed to Zealandia's wealth. Likewise, on land, they hunted birds—not for their meat, but for their feathers, which were a highly valuable commodity.

It is generally interesting that, just as on many later Polynesian islands, shells were used as a form of currency for trade in the Mu Culture. Zealandia thus served as a source of the Mu Culture's primary trading goods. Much of what we see in the petroglyphs here in the city indicates that the culture here was largely based on these luxury goods traded with the Mu Culture in the Pacific on the eastern side of Zealandia, and never developed an agricultural culture based on what Zealandia could provide. This might explain why the population vanished completely when the Mu Culture at sea disappeared. They could not transition to living off New Caledonia's resources. This city was located just on the warm side of New Caledonia's ridge, where the cold side was quite barren. This undoubtedly made it a trade center, where those from the cold side came to trade for luxury goods.

It seems that this trade continued for a very long time, and the stone tablets also appear to testify to the city's history. The stone tablets describe how members of the Mu Culture first flew over the mountain range and down to the warm side of Zealandia, where the buoyancy in their airships was reduced due to the warmer climate. Here they found a land full of many plants, colorful flowers, and animals. By the sea on the other side, they found a warm sea they could swim and dive in, quite different from the ice-filled sea. Here they learned to ride their trained whales, and in the sea, they found colorful corals that matched the vibrant land over the waves. However, they also found that this land did not provide the same abundant hunting as the cold, nutrient-rich sea, but the colorful shells and corals they found in abundance quickly became sought after by their peers in the Pacific, who were willing to trade their ample supplies for colorful feathered garments.

Thus, Zealandia became viable. This place was ideal for airships to land, so it soon became a trading post where abundant supplies were exchanged for colorful luxury goods.

This brought prosperity, and soon there were those who settled here and made feathered garments, shell necklaces, and much more. An actual city began to emerge with a permanent population. Those who caught birds for feathers and dived for corals came here to trade their goods for supplies, and those who engaged in hunting in the Pacific brought supplies to obtain feathered garments and coral necklaces.

This became a rich place for exchange that grew with the increasing trade, and soon the whale and seal skin tents were surrounded by stone buildings lifted into place by the airships. The city's wealth seemed endless, as the large population on the ice continent Mu had a great appetite for Zealandia's luxury goods. It was an exchange that lasted for generations.

Then we come to the stone tablets, which show that the development took a turn for the worse for the culture here on Zealandia. There is much evidence suggesting that the decline of the Whale Culture in the Pacific began here. Many petroglyphs depict storms that the whale culture feared as they were dangerous for their airships. Back when I found the late whale culture in Greenland, the storm was a feared symbol. However, it was not storms that damaged the city or Zealandia's flora and fauna initially. What is shown is that more precipitation fell as rain, and the ice cover on the eastern side began to break up more and more and was blown away, making the sea increasingly ice-free for longer periods. Simultaneously, the petroglyphs indicate that the warm and humid climate on New Caledonia's east side intensified, causing the tropical forests to expand toward the sea, which became warmer.

New Caledonia had thus begun to transition towards today's climate. The city here had still been able to supply all the luxury goods it always had, but with the ice cover disappearing and the warmer weather, it became harder for the airships to reach it as buoyancy decreased with the heat.

What we can read from the petroglyphs in general paints a picture of the Asian side of the Pacific's great ice sheet beginning to melt first. The ice cover along the equator from South America's Humboldt Current had started to melt before reaching all the way down along Zealandia's eastern coast. At the same time, the ice cover to the north along the Marianas and Japan had collapsed, as it was upheld by the Humboldt Current.

A retreat of the ice eastward towards America had thus begun, leaving Zealandia with a connection to the broader whale culture that had primarily moved south, where the ice cover around Antarctica persisted for a long time.

However, it quickly becomes clear from the petroglyphs that this was a very short-lived reprieve for the New Caledonian part of Zealandia. Zealandia is a very low-lying landmass, so with the rising sea levels, the land connection between New Caledonia and New Zealand was one of the first to be submerged, and the ice cover moved all the way down to New Zealand, leaving New Caledonia isolated.

The last tablets show the New Caledonian whale culture's efforts to maintain contact with their peers. The Pacific was still rich, so they could catch what they needed, but the heat was challenging for their hot air balloons.

In return, many reeds began to grow in the eastern swamps, which they started using to build gigantic floating islands, which could act like the ice once did, allowing them to live on the sea. Much like the reed islands of the Uru people known from Lake Titicaca in South America and the floating gardens in Mexico.

From the motifs in the petroglyphs, it appears that they took this to the extreme and set whale-skin balloons over the reed islands, allowing them to float and thus create islands in the sky, which could be towed by tame whales or moved slowly forward with whale oil.

It is a good example of technology pushed to its extreme in an environment where it was on its last legs. Much of what we see indicates that the Mu Culture here reached its peak in an attempt to simply build the world that was on the verge of being lost. The access to reeds allowed them to recreate the ice islands on which the whale culture had depended with plants. It even seems to have worked for a long period, where the Zealandian whale culture could thrive on its own terms.

It was sustainable as long as the rich water cycle in the Pacific during the ice age continued. It allowed for abundant hunting of whales and seals.

However, Zealandia was again at the forefront of decline. With the disappearance of the ice, the vertical oceanic pump also began to fail, and the exchange between surface water and bottom water dropped dramatically. The environment began to resemble the oceanic desert of our present-day southern Pacific. This was what the Mu Culture in New Caledonia could not handle! The petroglyphs speak clearly. The scorching sun leads to fewer and fewer whales and seals.

There are depictions of a migration southward to southern Zealandia. Some petroglyphs show a clear map of the reed islands' journey towards what is clearly the North Island of New Zealand, where the area near Auckland in the north seems to have been of interest as a destination. The locations are very clearly depicted by the ancient sculptor.

It seems that we will indeed head to New Zealand, but now we know where to look. After a few days of rest and resupply in Noumea, we set course for New Zealand.

We had taken pictures of the petroglyphs with maps showing where on New Zealand's North Island the Mu Culture from New Caledonia had emigrated to. We processed these pictures and maps of New Zealand's North Island through artificial intelligence and obtained some surprisingly accurate coordinates off the Auckland area.

Based on what we deduced from the petroglyphs, there was a massive wetland with an abundance of reeds at the time when the reed culture migrated there.

They specifically targeted an area that suited the way in which their branch of the whale culture had developed and that they wished to continue and further develop. They migrated south only after their prey had become insufficient at New Caledonia.

But with this migration, the culture that was focused on the pursuit of luxury goods like feathers in New Caledonia had also been lost. Only a modified version of the whale culture had survived on the reed islands.

I wonder if the whale culture adapted with reed islands elsewhere where there was access to reeds as the ice receded? It could possibly be the case in some places along the American Pacific coast. It might be worth investigating at a later date. There is no doubt that the majority of the whale culture from the ice continent Mu withdrew to the American coast as the ice continent collapsed. They could follow the ice all the way since new ice was constantly coming from the Humboldt Current.

The ice simply reached shorter and shorter distances into the Pacific. It must be a peculiar experience to slowly see your world melting away beneath your feet.

Now we are heading to a place where the Mu Culture tried to build their way out of the problem with reed islands. The petroglyphs had shown this place as the homeland of the reeds, so it must have had a much greater abundance of reeds than New Caledonia.

NEW ZEALAND

After a swift and successful journey south, we dock in Auckland, where we take a rest and seek some information about the sea where we will be diving. It's a point southeast of Auckland. The sea around New Zealand is much rougher than around New Caledonia, so it's wise to be well-prepared. We also ensure we wait for a good weather forecast for an extended period. We want no surprises while we're diving.

Once we feel everything is ready and the weather is favorable, we set sail for our next dive site. The question now is what we might hope to find down there. The reed culture was based on reed islands, so there's unlikely to be a city like in New Caledonia in the reed swamps that have been submerged here, but perhaps we can find some tablets with petroglyphs.

We descended into the depths and located the plain that must have been the reed swamp and began our search. It was met with no success. There was no sign of stone tablets or anything else in this long-lost reed swamp. We searched for several days but found nothing, so it was time to consider other options. We had also investigated a cliff face near the plain but found nothing there either. However, we decided to repeat the process from Kiritimati and photograph the entire cliff face, allowing the artificial intelligence to see if it could uncover anything.

We proceeded systematically, taking overview pictures of the cliff as well as many close-ups of the surface. The water was dark and overgrown here, so it was not easy for us to see. It was clear that we had come to a different sea than that closer to the equator. It resembled more the Aleutians.

Once we had taken the photos, we set the diving equipment aside and let the artificial intelligence start its work. Now we could only wait and see what it would reveal.

Meanwhile, we enjoyed the view of this southern and cooler sea with the North Island in the background. There was something wild and untamed about it, even though Auckland was not far away. It shows that you can be quite close to civilization and still feel far from human traces. I wonder how little it would take to erase our traces when the whale culture's traces have been so easily erased? How enduring are our buildings, when it comes down to it?

As I pondered these thoughts, the processing of our images was completed.

There was a hit! Look at that. We were right next to the traces of the whale culture and couldn't sense them!

It was a cliff with petroglyphs similar to those I had seen from East Greenland in the past. However, the history of this place quickly reveals itself to be brief. When the reed culture had established itself here, the ice had already retreated to the South Island, making the reed culture constantly the rear guard for the whale culture's retreat from the western Pacific.

They are the farthest tip of a small branch of the whale culture that extends from the South Pacific ice cover to New Zealand. The rest of the whale culture had retreated to the west coast of America and the Aleutians to the north.

The reed culture continued to diverge from the culture on the ice cover, as they became increasingly dependent on staying on and hunting from their reed islands.

However, the problem was that they were thus dependent on this area with many reeds to continually maintain their reed islands, while the whale culture in the south simply followed the ice.

It also appears from the petroglyphs that the distance to their relatives in the south was constantly increasing as the ice retreated further south towards the tip of the South Island, while the reed culture was trapped where they had access to reeds.

There are fewer and fewer whale tail petroglyphs in the later petroglyphs. This is a clear sign that the culture's foundation is disappearing.

There are petroglyphs showing groups leaving the reed culture to join the whale culture further south, while some stubbornly cling to life on the reed islands. They increasingly begin to hunt birds and seals, as the whales become fewer, and they also disappear as tame animals used for riding and towing the reed islands.

However, they still use airships powered by seal oil, as it is also suitable for it. However, it is an increasingly impoverished culture as the sea also becomes poorer. It is evident from the petroglyphs that formerly readily available resources are beginning to become scarce, and thus attempts are made to create substitutes for these.

The most evident is the blubber lamps, which the whale culture traditionally made by hollowing out whale bones to form an efficient double-chamber burner with fuel around an inner tube, where the air for combustion and the exhaust for buoyancy could pass through. With the increasing shortage of whales as prey, the reed culture had to become exceedingly creative. It appears that they had developed a form of ceramics in the process. Something I had never seen before in the whale culture, which only very rarely used land-based resources for high processing, but the culture on Zealandia had naturally been different.

According to the petroglyphs, they used a curved trunk from a smaller tree and shaped clay around it with many sticks through the clay to create air vents. They then fired it all, leaving only the burned perforated clay tubes. Afterward, they applied a layer of blubber around this tube and shaped clay around the blubber, which was then fired again. This resulted in an outer and inner tube that fit together and had a bend at one end to direct the incoming air.

In this way, the reed culture could continue to use blubber lamps for both propulsion and buoyancy in their airships, even though whales had become rare. They became more dependent on seals for skin for the balloons as well.

It is impressive how much they managed to adapt their culture to the new conditions. It allowed them to remain in the reed forests longer while the ice and the rest of the whale culture retreated southward.

However, they faced a central problem brought about by the disappearance of the ice. The whale culture traditionally obtained water by melting ice. This was no longer an option since they lived on the sea on their reed islands; they had to go ashore to collect fresh water. This was a significant task that required a lot of effort and time.

Yet, they found a solution in line with their cultural traditions. The petroglyphs depict large triangular sails, with one end anchored to a container on the ground while the other two ends were held up by airships when the reed island had to be moved. With these sails, they could capture dew from the air and thereby obtain water. Naturally, this could only be done in calm winds. Additionally, it was fuel-intensive if the sail was to be held up by airships, which only made sense when moving the reed islands. It seems to have been a starting point, however. Later, they began to fell trunks from smaller trees on land, just as they harvested reeds from the swamps on land.

These branches and trunks were then used to hold sails so they could collect water from the morning mist each day. It is amazing how the reed culture managed to adapt as well as possible to their situation.

However, the amount of water they could obtain this way was much more modest compared to what the ice had once provided, so it was again a culture that had to conserve resources compared to the past. The reed culture was incredibly adept at adapting, but it constantly struggled against time, living at a time when their world was collapsing around them. The ice continued to recede more and more, and there are petroglyphs depicting the dreadful day when the burning warm god caused the ice to lose its connection to New Zealand's South Island, thus separating the reed culture from the rest of the whale culture. From then on, it was only possible to maintain contact with airships over open sea to the ice cover in the south.

It is evident that the connection became progressively worse. However, the reed culture held on and continued their new lifestyle on self-built islands until the final catastrophe occurred. Zealandia is a low-lying landmass, so the sea level rise impacted here first, which early on separated New Zealand from New Caledonia and thereby destroyed the production of ice masses. Even the areas close to New Zealand, like the large reed swamps, were early victims of the sea, while large ice masses were still present on land.

The reed swamps began to be swallowed by the sea, thus removing the very basis for the reed culture. Without a persistent source of reeds, they could no longer maintain their life on the sea. This placed them in a situation with two options: either to go ashore or emigrate south to join their relatives in Antarctica, who still had a connection to the Humboldt current and thus up along the west coast of South America, where there was still a foundation for the whale culture.

It appears that the reed culture made the decision to move south. The petroglyphs depict more and more reed islands embarking on a journey southward to find solid ice beneath their feet. Thus, the whale culture in the Pacific had retreated towards the Antarctic ice sheet in the south, the Arctic in the north, and along the coast of South America by the Humboldt Current in the east. In this way, the Mu culture on the ice continent had been doomed by the ice simply vanishing beneath their feet, and the reed culture remained as the last remnant, clinging to their former hunting grounds with immense ingenuity. However, ultimately, everything turned against them, and they too had to follow the ice into an increasingly harsher environment far from the equator, to a place where half the year is dark. We must assume that the descendants of the reed culture and their relatives, who stayed on the ice, followed the ice edge along the Antarctic Ocean and up along the west coast of South America in search of better conditions.

In any case, the trail of the reed culture ends here. They had returned to the whale culture on the ice. This is what we could interpret from the petroglyphs here at the now submerged reed swamps. A culture that branched off from the Mu culture only to eventually return to the whale culture. They were too tied to the sea to choose to go ashore. Their culture was too focused on hunting sea creatures.

My search for the whale culture has now taken us through the Pacific from north to south. We have found traces of the whale culture that I never thought possible when we set out from the Aleutians to Japan and the Yonaguni Monument.

Based on what we have found, the whale culture at its peak is identical to the lost continent of Mu, which turns out to have been a continent of ice maintained by the Humboldt Current in the middle of the Pacific, far from all the continents of stone and dirt. Not only that, but on Zealandia, the Mu culture existed as an actual city-building civilization on a continent that was truly sinking into the sea.

This mighty culture existed long before the known cultures of historical times and was contemporaneous with the Ice Age hunter-gatherers of the Eurasian mammoth steppe. The whale culture came from here but replaced the mammoth with whales. With the Mu culture, the whale culture reached an impressively high level without ever being anything other than a hunter-gatherer society. They were able to maintain such an advanced culture based on hunting due to the enormous abundance of prey in the form of whales, provided by the unique sea conditions in the Pacific during the Ice Age. This allowed the Mu culture to achieve a very high stage and fill the sky over the Ice Age Pacific with airships made from whale materials. A technology that the whale culture would preserve long after its disappearance in the Pacific and right up until its last outpost in East Greenland during the Holocene Maximum, as I wrote about in "The Whale Culture in Greenland"!

The whale culture disappeared from the Pacific as the ice, which was the basis of their culture, retreated. But it did so gradually and towards the west coast of South America, where the Humboldt Current brings cold water up from Antarctica.

It therefore seems clear to me that our search for the further development of the Mu culture should lead us to the coasts of Ecuador and Peru, where the Nazca Lines suggest a connection to the geoglyphs of the Mu culture. This is the goal of my further investigations. So, the next step will be to explore more about the whale culture in South America, where we will sail along the Pacific coast. For now, we will head home to prepare for our next adventure and work with what we have learned on this journey. Then we will see what stories can be found in South America!